LOST LEGENDS PRESENTS: THE QUEEN'S HERO

Roger Batista

Roger Batista

ISBN: 978-1-966642-50-3

Roger Batista

Dedication

With deep gratitude, this book is dedicated to

Michael and Gianna,

whose eager ears and shining eyes gave my stories a place to live.

May you always carry those tales with you,

just as I carry the joy of telling them.

*And to **Maria,***

whose patience has weathered countless rewrites,

and whose support has always been the quiet rhythm behind every word.

Table of Contents

About the Author

Roger Batista has been dancing with words since college — mostly unnoticed by the world, but not by the muse. A lifelong poet and storyteller, Roger's writing is known for its layered metaphors and unexpected humor, often described as tredaphoric — a metaphor within a metaphor, spiraling toward revelation.

His debut work of epic fantasy was born from a single song: a hero's whisper to a queen became a world, and a lyric became a legend. With themes of hidden identity, loyalty, and the timeless search for self, Roger's work invites readers to lose and find themselves — often in the same sentence.

He currently lives in Florida, where he divides his time between imagining worlds and asking, "What if this story already happened... and we just forgot?"

Prologue: The Tredaphor

In the beginning, there was the shadow, then the dream. There, in the silence between breath and thought, the world first took shape. The realms of men, of gods, of beasts, and of the forgotten ones—the echoes of their voices in the wind, carried across forgotten mountains—have always been entangled in the web of myth, where truth is as elusive as the very stars themselves.

I, the one who watches, cloaked in mystery, come to you now not to tell you a tale, but to invite you into a riddle. A riddle not yet solved. The riddles of the universe are often like this: no answer is given without the price of your trust. And yet, trust in nothing as easily as you trust in the darkness of your own heart.

The Tredaphor. What is it? Is it salvation, or is it a weapon? You will find that the very answer is both—and neither. It is a concept that dwells in the cracks between worlds, where dreams brush against reality, where shadows reveal secrets too dangerous to behold.

Do you believe in fate? I know you do, for you are human. Yet I say to you, do not trust the obvious hero, for he is but a mirror held up to deceive you. A hero's strength is often his greatest flaw, and in his wake, destruction will find fertile soil. In this land of eight kingdoms, where empires rise and fall with the tide of time, there are those who seek salvation and those who seek power. And yet, I warn you, the path you walk is neither one of light nor of darkness—it is one of paradox.

There is a prophecy, a whispered secret that clings to the bones of this world: **The Day of Brothers True.** Two brothers, bound by blood and fate, will come to reshape the future. They are bound not in friendship, but in competition, for only one can claim the prize that awaits. A crown, a throne, a legacy—these are the things they will fight for. And yet, neither the crown nor the throne will decide the fate of the kingdoms.

You see, the tredaphor is not a weapon of war—it is a weapon of faith. It is a weapon that will either bind you to salvation or break you apart. It will not choose you; you will choose it, whether you realize it or not. And so, in the days to come, you must watch. You must listen. And you must understand that the one who seems most destined for greatness is often the one who has already lost his way. And perhaps, the one who seems most unworthy is the one who will redeem you.

I will not ask you to follow a path I have not already walked. My journey was not one of joy nor of glory. I, too, sought the answers to the riddles of the world. But you must beware—the truth is not so simple. The truth is often an illusion, something you cannot see until it is too late.

The Day of Brothers True draws near, and the destinies of Falco, Cade, Travis, and the others are intertwined with the very fate of the kingdoms. You will hear their names, see their faces, and wonder—are they the heroes they claim to be? Or are they pawns in a game played by forces beyond their understanding?

The winds are shifting, and the day will come when the fate of all rests not in the hands of kings, but in the hands of those who choose not to rule. When the time comes, remember this: the Tredaphor is not what it appears. Trust no one—least of all, the one who calls himself the hero.

The shadows stir, and the riddle grows deeper. Step carefully. The day is coming when the truth will be revealed—not in the way you expect, but in the way you fear most. But remember this: every end is simply the beginning of a new question.

Chapter 1 – Falco

The arrow flew before the deer heard it. A faint whisper of wind, a blink of instinct—and it was done.

Falco stood still in the clearing, his eyes locked not on the fallen stag, but on the trees beyond it, as if expecting something else to emerge. He listened. Wind. Branches creaking. Crows shifting. Nothing more.

"You didn't even give it a chance," came a voice behind him, light with jest. "That's the third one this week. You trying to make the forest extinct?"

Falco glanced over his shoulder to see Multir approaching, his tall frame cloaked in moss-stained leathers, bow slung across his back. A rabbit dangled from his hand.

"They move too slowly," Falco replied, his tone flat. "Or maybe I just see too quickly."

"Or maybe you're just bored," Multir said. "You always get like this when there's no real threat. Restless as a caged wolf."

Falco shrugged and knelt beside the deer. His hands moved with practiced reverence as he began the necessary rites. The blood ran warm over his fingers. There was no joy in the kill, but neither sorrow. Only rhythm. Purpose. A job well done.

Multir watched in silence before speaking again. "Travis said he saw you pacing the ridge last night. Didn't sleep?"

"I did. But I dreamed."

Multir's brow furrowed. "The same one?"

Falco nodded, lips tight. "But clearer this time. There were more of them. They wore white armor with no crest. And they knelt."

Multir crouched beside him. "Knelt before you?"

A pause.

"Yes."

The two were quiet. Only the wind filled the space between their words. Somewhere above, a crow cawed, hoarse and distant.

"What did the voice say this time?" Multir asked.

Falco looked away. "It said, *'It is almost time… they are waiting.'*"

Multir was no fool, and he'd known Falco since they were boys—back when climbing trees and scraping knees was the most danger they faced. Their childhood had been filled with the kind of reckless joy that only came from growing up in the wild outskirts of Bethos, where the forests stretched endlessly and parents called from doorways at dusk, hoping their sons hadn't wandered too far. Even then, Falco had a quiet intensity about him, a stillness that hinted at something deeper. While the other boys played games of pretend and roughhoused in the fields, Falco listened—to the wind, to the birds, to the silences between sounds.

Multir had watched his friend pick up a sword for the first time at fourteen and move with a grace and precision that defied logic. It hadn't been training—it had been instinct. Falco didn't just learn quickly; it was as if he remembered. Later, when the elders sent them out to track game in the hills, Falco had followed prints no one else could see, spotting patterns in the undergrowth like he was reading a book. He could move through brush without a sound and climb cliff faces that made seasoned hunters blanch. More than once, Multir had turned to find Falco staring off into the distance, brow furrowed, moments before something happened—a storm, a landslide, a stranger arriving in camp.

Falco was different. There was no denying it. He carried something inside him that even he didn't seem to understand, something old and powerful. And different things, in Bethos,

11

were often feared. In a place where tradition held tightly to the past and mystery was met with suspicion, Falco's gifts made him both extraordinary—and dangerous in the eyes of those who refused to understand him.

"You should tell Travis," Multir said gently. "You know how he is with puzzles and prophecies. He lives for this sort of madness."

Falco tied off the last of the cords securing the deer and stood. "He'll just make it worse. He always does."

Multir smirked. "That's true. But he means well."

They began the walk back to the outskirts of Fenwall, the quiet village where they lived, hugging the edge of the western woods. The road was soft with damp leaves, and the afternoon light broke through the branches in slow golden shafts.

"You ever think about it?" Falco asked suddenly. "Why I can do the things I can?"

"All the time," Multir said. "But I figured if you didn't have an answer, there's no use in me guessing. You're either blessed or cursed. Or both."

Falco kicked a loose stone from the path. "Feels more like a curse lately."

They walked on in silence, the forest falling away to the hills beyond. The crumbling tower of Fenwall Keep peeked above the horizon—half collapsed from an old war no one bothered to remember.

By the time they reached Travis's stone cottage, the scent of ink, wax, and pine hit their noses. Travis had once considered joining the military academy, but instead became something far more dangerous: a thinker.

Falco pushed the heavy wooden door open without knocking, his boots scuffing softly against the stone floor. "We brought food," he announced, holding up a wrapped bundle that gave off the aroma of roasted meat and herbs.

"No need," came Travis's voice from deeper inside the cluttered room. "I'm already feasting. On madness."

Falco and Multir exchanged a look before stepping inside. The space was dimly lit, lit only by the soft glow of candle stubs and the occasional flicker from a smoldering hearth. They found Travis hunched over a desk nearly collapsing under the weight of ancient scrolls, cracked leather-bound tomes, and several pieces of what looked suspiciously like dried lizard skin or some other unsettling specimen. Ink stains marked his fingers, and a half-finished diagram curled off the side of the table.

"You need fresh air," Multir muttered, wrinkling his nose at the musty, acrid smell that clung to the room like smoke.

"I need answers," Travis snapped back, not looking up. "And guess what? I may have one."

He finally turned toward them, eyes bright with a kind of manic energy, his spectacles sliding down his nose. He froze, catching sight of Falco's face. "Another dream?"

Falco nodded.

"Same white-armored men? Same cryptic nonsense?"

Falco nodded again.

Travis stood and began pacing, gesturing like a man assembling invisible puzzle pieces. "I think it's connected. All of it. The dreams. The state of Bethos. The Queen's disappearance from court. The whispers in the capital. Falco, I think—"

"No," Falco cut him off. "Don't say it."

Travis stopped. "You don't even know what I was going to say."

"You think I'm the hero of some prophecy," Falco said, voice sharp. "That these dreams are destiny, and I'm chosen for something grand."

Travis blinked. "Well… yes."

Falco crossed his arms. "Do you know what that means, if you're right? War. Betrayal. Death. Heroes die, Travis."

"Not always."

"They do. Eventually."

Multir spoke up from the doorframe. "Still… if something is coming, shouldn't we understand it? Whether or not you believe you're part of it?"

Falco didn't respond. His eyes had drifted to a page on Travis's desk. A map. But not of Bethos. Or not exactly. This one had lines drawn where none should be—markings of rivers that hadn't flowed in years, cities that were supposed to be ruins, and a small, glowing symbol in the far east. A circle split in two.

"What's that?" Falco asked, pointing.

Travis followed his gaze. "That… that's what I was working on. It's the sigil of the old House Daemir. The ones who ruled the Greens before the crown fell. I think it ties to the old legends of the Tredaphor."

Falco narrowed his eyes. "That word again. You used it last week."

"And I'll keep using it," Travis said. "Because it's important. The Tredaphor—some say it was a sword, others say a crown. But none agree on its nature. One scroll even calls it 'the salvation of fools, the weapon of kings.'"

Multir looked skeptical. "That sounds like a metaphor. Or a drunk poet."

"Or prophecy," Travis replied, lowering his voice. "There's mention of a day—The Day of Brothers True. A nameless hero. A trial that splits the realm. I think it's starting. I think Falco's dreams are the beginning."

Falco turned away. He wanted to laugh, but something in his chest ached instead. That voice—*they are waiting*—echoed again.

That night, back in his room above the village's abandoned mill, Falco sat on the roof beneath a sky bruised with stars. He had hoped to find silence, but dreams did not wait for sleep anymore.

He stared at the moon, a silver coin suspended in ink, and thought of the white-armored men. Of the kneeling. Of the cryptic voice.

He had not told them everything.

In the latest dream, there had been a shadow. Taller than the rest. Watching him. Behind the kneeling men, unmoving. Its eyes had glowed like embers. And when it spoke, the others fell silent.

"You will choose, but not once. You will kill, but not with hatred. You will fall, and still rise. But if you reach for the crown, it will turn to ash."

Falco closed his eyes and whispered the words into the wind, like a prayer or a curse.

The wind answered—briefly—through the trees. Leaves shifted like whispers in a council chamber. And for a moment, Falco thought he saw movement beneath the moonlight. A flicker of white. A shimmer of steel.

But when he rose, bow ready, the clearing was empty.

Just the wind.

Just the night.

Or so it seemed.

Chapter 2 – The Eight Kingdoms

They say the world was once whole—a single breath of land under a single sky, shaped by the silent hand of the Maker. Mountains rose where the Maker pressed a finger; rivers ran where the Maker traced a line. It was a time of unity, of one people beneath the sun, before time, like fire through parchment, split it apart. The sundered lands scattered, drifting like embers in a windstorm.

Kingdoms rose like waves, brilliant and brief, and crashed the same, lost to war, greed, or the weight of their own ambition. Now, only eight remain—eight kingdoms isolated and unsure, each clinging to crumbling histories and fading songs. No one remembers the world before the fall. No one remembers what was lost.

And so, the world is a shattered mirror—each shard a kingdom, each reflecting its own truth, its own version of what was, and none able to see the whole ever again.

The Kingdom of Bethos stood at the western heart of the realm, nestled between the Ashen Hills and the Cloudmere Sea. Once, it was a beacon of law and learning, ruled by scholars and statesmen who traced their lineage back to Adriun the First—King, prophet, and, some whispered, the last to speak with the gods.

But those days had slipped into myth, and Bethos now teetered on the edge of collapse.

Its once-gleaming cities grew tarnished beneath layers of grime and neglect. Roads that had once echoed with the steady march of knights and the measured stride of robed judges now teemed with thieves, smugglers, and worse— predators who ruled by fear rather than law. The High Council of Lords, cloistered in the soaring stone chambers of the Capitol Spire, bickered endlessly, their voices swollen with privilege, their intentions rotted by self-interest. Taxation surged without reason, draining the commons dry, while trade slowed to a crawl. In the east, cracked soil yielded nothing under a relentless drought; in the west, fields drowned beneath unceasing rain.

And at the center of this growing storm stood a Queen no one saw.

They called her The Silent Crown. Some whispered she had gone mad, others that she was long dead. Yet her decrees continued—always written, never spoken—bearing the twisted rose of House Mirelin.

Whispers flowed through taverns and barracks alike: she possessed *the last blessing of Adriun*—a relic or a curse, none knew which. It was said she could dream the future, or shift it. That her dreams turned to storms. That her silence was not madness, but power.

"Bethos stands because she sleeps," said one saying.

"Bethos falls because she wakes," said another.

In the taverns of Fenwall and the courts of the capital, the name of *Vladrin* was rising. General Vladrin, commander of the Iron Watch, had seized authority in the Queen's absence. He spoke of order and tradition, and of purging the "foreign blood" corrupting Bethos' legacy. The people, desperate and hungry, began to cheer him. But others saw in his rise the return of tyranny—of blades in shadows and voices silenced.

Far to the east, across the Bleeding Marshes and the Shattered Spine Mountains, sprawled **The Greens**—a land without a king, without borders, and without peace.

There, the world pulsed like a half-remembered dream.

Forests that moved when unobserved. Rivers that reversed their flow. Trees that whispered names into the ears of sleeping children. Crops that grew overnight and withered just as quickly.

And beneath it all, a heartbeat.

Thump. Thump. Thump.

"Wake up," the wind sometimes hissed.

"You're dreaming."

In the Greens, belief bent reality. Cities rose and fell like breathing. Leaders claimed dominion only to vanish days later, their names forgotten. The land did not obey maps or minds. It obeyed only itself.

But men, ever proud, still fought for it.

Eight generals ruled eight factions, each declaring themselves the true heir of the Greens. Their pride ran deep, and so did their hunger for power. They built citadels of stone and bone, monuments to their ambition and madness. Around these strongholds gathered armies—zealots drunk on prophecy, beasts twisted by ancient rites, soldiers who knew no fear. Their banners flapped defiantly in the wind as they marched to war. But the war never ended. It only changed shape, spreading like a sickness across the land.

Amidst the chaos, something stirred—something older than kings, older than Bethos itself. The ground beneath the soldiers' feet began to hum with unnatural rhythm. The skies, once silent, cracked with emerald lightning, though no storms passed. And the voices—those voices—grew louder. Whispering. Calling. Not just to the generals, but to the land itself, as if awakening something that had only pretended to sleep.

"Thump. Thump. Thump."

"Wake up…"

In the village of Korra Hollow, a child awoke screaming, claiming he saw a crown with no wearer and a throne of vines. In the ruins of Eld Braen, a woman disappeared into a mirror that showed only her shadow. And in the deepwood temple of Ashten'ka, monks awoke to find their sacred texts rewritten—new lines etched in ink that shimmered like oil: *"He who wears the tredaphor shall not seek it."*

Beyond the great players—Bethos and The Greens—six other kingdoms sprawled across the known lands, each burdened by its own curse.

Thermeldor, the Stonehold, ruled by its Guildlords and Forgemasters, was a city carved into mountain spires, ever at war with gravity and ambition. Its forges burned night and day, shaping weapons for whomever could pay the price.

Syrithin, the River Kingdom, where law was traded like coin and assassins walked as openly as merchants. The people spoke in riddles and truths alike, for in Syrithin, it was said, the truth could be bought—if you could afford the lie it buried.

Erekos, the Silent Waste, where sandstorms danced like specters and buried cities whispered through dunes. A desert of memory. A prison for those who fled prophecy.

Velshar, the Skyreach, where the last dragons were said to slumber in cliffs taller than clouds. Here, temples floated, anchored by tether and song, and monks debated the meaning of existence with birds that spoke back.

Noctir, the Black Vale, blanketed in endless night—its people pale, reclusive, and fiercely devout. They worshipped not the Maker, but the Echo—the memory of creation. Their dreams were said to bleed.

Miraen, the Shattered Coast, a kingdom in pieces—its islands spread like spilled pearls, ruled by pirate-kings and exiled princes. It was a land of exile and rebirth, where those cast out could rise again.

Yet none of these kingdoms stirred the winds of prophecy. None cast as long a shadow as Bethos or as strange a light as the Greens.

In the royal library beneath the Capitol Spire of Bethos, Cade—young, quiet, and ever-curious—ran his fingers along the spines of forbidden texts.

A book slid free with the whisper of old secrets.

The Tredaphor: Symbol, Curse, Salvation?

Cade opened it carefully. Its ink shimmered faintly in the candlelight. The pages were dense with riddles, half-legible prophecies, and illustrations of strange devices—crowns that split like seeds, swords shaped like questions.

He paused on one line, underlined twice.

"It cannot be given. It cannot be taken. The tredaphor reveals itself only to the unseen."

His fingers trembled.

From the hallway, he heard a voice—calm, clipped.

"You're not authorized to be here."

Cade turned to see a cloaked figure—one of the Queen's Silent Guard.

"I'm only reading," he said carefully.

The guard tilted their head. "What you read can shape what you become."

Cade met their gaze. "And what if I don't know what I am?"

The figure regarded him in silence, then turned and walked away, leaving Cade with the book, and more questions than answers.

In a northern forest clearing, a half-dozen men in ash-gray armor knelt silently before a figure cloaked in shadows. Above them, trees swayed without wind. The sky flickered.

"Is it time?" one asked.

The figure didn't speak. Only raised a hand.

From the woods came a soft beat.

Thump. Thump. Thump.

The trees whispered. *"They are waking."*

And in the Queen's Tower, where no servant dared linger, the woman called Mirelin sat before a tall mirror, her reflection covered in veil and flicker.

She spoke to no one, yet her voice filled the chamber.

"They gather. The Day draws near."

The mirror shimmered. A shape moved within it.

"I see them both," she whispered. "One with the eyes of the storm. One with the heart of glass. One will break. One will bleed. But neither shall be king."

She placed a hand upon the mirror, and it pulsed faintly, like a heartbeat.

Thump. Thump.

The Eight Kingdoms teetered on the edge of fate, each unaware of how closely they brushed against myth. The tredaphor, whatever it was, had begun to stir in the fabric of their stories, a ripple that would become a wave. Some would seek it, driven by desperation or power. Some would fear it, sensing only its shadow.

And some would carry it unknowingly, bearing a burden they could not name. But none would escape it. Not Bethos, crumbling under the weight of history and ambition, its halls echoing with forgotten oaths.

Not the Greens, alive with secrets and screaming dreams, where nothing grew that did not bite. Not the boy with the cursed gift, who could not close his eyes without opening another's pain. Not the other boy, who watched himself in mirrors and wondered which reflection would betray him first. The tredaphor was coming, and the kingdoms would remember its name.

Roger Batista

Chapter 3 – The Second of Two

Cade often wondered if something within him had fractured—not all at once, but slowly, like ice splintering beneath warm breath. It wasn't a dramatic break, not the kind that leaves scars or screams, but a subtle yielding, an invisible shift deep within. He could never pinpoint when it began. Perhaps it had always been there, dormant, waiting for the right pressure to bring the first fault line to light. Or perhaps it had started with a word spoken carelessly, a glance held too long, or the sudden stillness in a once-familiar place.

The others did not notice it. They saw only a quiet youth with thoughtful eyes and a penchant for wandering libraries and listening more than speaking. He was not the kind to draw attention. He asked a few questions, offered fewer answers. In Bethos, among the restless sons of noble houses and the would-be revolutionaries whispering in the alleys, Cade was easily overlooked. The tutors marked him as diligent but unremarkable. The palace guards noted him as obedient. Even his peers, ever drawn to drama and defiance, paid him little mind. And Cade preferred it that way. Silence gave him room to observe others and himself.

And that, perhaps, was why the visions came to him.

They never came to sleep. No dreams carried them. Instead, they arrived during moments of stillness, piercing through the veil of the ordinary. They came in the shimmer of torchlight on a polished suit of armor, in the hush of still water in the royal gardens, in the reflection of his own face within the black lacquer of a courtroom floor. There was no sound, no voice to accompany them. Only a shift—barely perceptible—that changed the way light moved, or how his skin prickled, or how a shadow lingered too long. And always, always, he knew when it was not merely a reflection, but something else watching him back. It was not imagination. It was not fear. It was presence. And it knew him.

The first time it happened, he had been thirteen.

He'd wandered, half in a daze, into the Queen's reflecting pool—an off-limits place of manicured hedges and perfect quiet, hidden behind marble walls and guarded by the weight of ancient tradition. It was the sort of place spoken of in hushed tones, where no one went without purpose or permission.

Even the air had felt different there. Heavy. Waiting. The garden was always in bloom, lilies blossoming regardless of season, their white petals untouched by insects or decay. Not even the birds sang within that circle of silence.

The water in the pool was unnaturally still. Not a ripple stirred it. The breeze that moved the trees beyond the hedges did not reach here. It was like looking into a pane of black glass.

He'd leaned over the edge, idly, his reflection the last thing on his mind—until he saw it. Not his face, but a throne of carved bone, pale and gleaming like ivory. And seated on it, himself, older, taller, more severe. His robes shimmered as if woven from threads of sunlight and shadow intertwined, shifting with impossible texture. A crown rested upon his brow, thin and sharp, as if hammered from gold until it bled.

But it wasn't the strange finery that seized him. It was the face. His face. Cold. Triumphant. And horribly, utterly alone.

Then the image changed.

The throne was gone. Now he knelt in dust and shadow. His robes were torn. His hands were covered in blood.

And before him, Falco. Pale. Wounded. Silent. A sword lay across his knees, as if awaiting judgment.

Then a voice had come, smooth and quiet, like silk slipping over glass:

"You will follow the wrong one. And still, you'll lead."

He'd stumbled back in shock, heart pounding, as a gardener came running, shouting about trespass. But Cade barely heard.

The words rang in his head. They never stopped.

Six years passed.

The visions continued.

He kept them secret. Even from Falco.

Especially from Falco.

He now sat alone in the chamber of mirrors, far beneath the Bethosian cathedral.

Few knew it existed. Fewer entered. It was a remnant of the old faith—a place of reflection, literally and spiritually, where acolytes once sought the divine through the infinite repetition of self. Now it was disused. Dust choked the corners. The candles sputtered when you dared light them.

But Cade came here often.

In the center of the room was a mirrored pedestal, and above it, a great circular dome of glass that reflected every movement a hundred times over. Cade stood beneath it now, arms folded, gaze fixed on the mirror.

"Show me," he whispered.

Nothing moved.

Then—slowly—the image changed.

No longer his own face, but *two figures*, walking side by side across a ruined bridge. One tall and broad, a hunter's bow slung across his back. The other thinner, draped in a scholar's cloak.

"Falco," Cade breathed.

The mirror pulsed faintly.

The figures came to a fork in the path. One road led toward a gleaming citadel. The other descended into a chasm veiled in fog.

The taller figure—the one like Falco—pointed to the citadel. The other hesitated. And then, slowly, *followed.*

"You will follow the wrong one."

The voice returned, cool and knowing.

"And still, you'll lead."

32

The image warped. Smoke rose. Screams echoed faintly. And for just a moment, Cade saw himself again— not as a boy, but as a man in chains, standing above a city in flames, holding a crown he did not want.

He closed his eyes.

"I don't understand," he whispered. "What am I meant to do?"

The mirror said nothing. Only shimmered. And in the shimmer, his own uncertain face stared back.

Later that evening, he met with Falco and Travis in a forgotten courtyard tucked between the archives and the royal kitchens.

Falco was pacing, restless energy rippling off him in waves. Travis sat with a map unrolled on a stone bench, his fingers smudged with ink and dust.

"You're late," Falco said, without looking up.

"I was thinking," Cade replied evenly, settling onto the bench beside Travis.

"You're always thinking." Falco stopped, turned. "Have you ever tried *doing*?"

Travis chuckled. "And what would you have him do? Wrestle a dream?"

Falco ignored him. His eyes were on Cade now, sharp and questioning. "You've been... strange lately."

Cade raised an eyebrow. "Only lately?"

"You know what I mean."

Cade hesitated. He could lie, but he was tired. And the truth, even in fragments, was clawing its way out.

"I've been seeing things."

That quieted both of them.

Falco stepped closer. "Visions?"

Cade nodded slowly. "Through reflections. Mirrors, water, glass. It's not just imagination. I've seen... futures. Or possible ones."

Falco's face hardened. "And what do these 'visions' say?"

Cade looked away. "They don't speak clearly. Just riddles. Warnings."

"About what?"

Cade hesitated again.

"You. Me. Us. A choice. A path. A throne."

Falco's brow furrowed. "A throne?"

Travis leaned in. "Bethos doesn't even have a visible monarch. Are you saying—"

"I don't know what I'm saying," Cade snapped. "Only that it feels important. Like something is watching. Waiting."

Falco folded his arms. "And you're just now telling us?"

Cade met his gaze. "Would you have believed me if I'd told you sooner?"

A long silence.

Falco's anger softened into something quieter. "No," he admitted. "Probably not."

That night, Cade wandered the eastern gardens, his thoughts spiraling like leaves in the wind. The moon cast broken silver across the fountains. He paused near the old reflecting pool—the same one from years before.

He leaned over it again.

No vision came.

Just his face. Tired. Pale. Real.

But then, a voice behind him.

"You seek answers in glass?"

He turned sharply.

A woman stood behind him, draped in travel-stained robes. Her face was partially veiled, and her eyes glimmered like polished stone, gray with hints of violet.

"I—who are you?" he asked.

"Someone who listens," she said.

"To what?"

"To the water. To the mirrors. To the silence."

Cade frowned. "You're not from the palace."

"No. But I've walked its edges."

She stepped beside him and peered into the pool.

"The reflections show truths. But not all truths belong to you. Some are borrowed."

"What does that mean?"

"It means you may be seeing through more than your own eyes."

Cade swallowed. "You know about the tredaphor."

The woman's lips curled slightly.

"I know enough to fear it."

"Tell me what it is."

She reached into the pool. Her hand touched the surface but did not ripple it.

"The tredaphor is not a thing. Not exactly. It is a truth that cannot be touched. A choice that cannot be made willingly. A power that dies the moment it's claimed."

Cade's voice was a whisper. "Then who holds it?"

She turned to him.

"Perhaps the one who follows. Perhaps the one who leads. Perhaps... both."

And just like that, she was gone.

No footsteps. No sound.

Just an empty garden and the still water.

Back in his chambers, Cade stood before the mirror once more.

His reflection was normal.

And yet—it smiled before he did.

He dreamed, at last.

But not as himself.

He was someone else, watching from a distance as **Falco** stood on a high cliff, speaking to an unseen crowd.

The wind tore at his cloak. His face was older, harder. The sky behind him burned orange with dawn.

"We are not born heroes," Falco said. "We are made in the moments between pain and purpose."

The crowd cheered.

Then silence.

Cade stepped forward—but his voice was gone.

He opened his mouth to warn them.

To say: *He isn't the one.*

But the dream melted like wax.

He awoke breathless, hands shaking.

The mirror across the room shimmered faintly.

In the tower, the Queen—still silent, still unseen—stood before her own mirror, watching something Cade could not.

"He sees," she whispered.

"But what will he *do*?"

Chapter 4 – Fire Before the Flood

The night the palace burned, the stars vanished.

Bethos had always been a city of order—its streets aligned like the teeth of a comb, its towers rising with dignified restraint. From its founding, every stone had been placed with purpose, every gate opened and closed according to centuries-old tradition. The city prided itself on its predictability, its symmetry, and its calm governance. But that night, the sky itself seemed to recoil, cloaking the city in a darkness deeper than mere absence of light. No moon, no stars—only smoke and the terrible orange glow.

Cade stood atop the eastern wall, the wind tugging at his cloak, his eyes fixed on the ruin unfolding below. The royal palace, once the anchor of Bethos's solemn grandeur, was an inferno. Flames licked the heavens, casting grotesque shadows that danced across the city's stone facades. Once-sturdy windows burst outward with sharp cracks, coughing sparks into the air like dying breaths.

The scent of burning cedar and old parchment filled the air, mingling with the acrid tang of fear. Cade could taste it on his tongue, feel it in his chest. Somewhere beneath the roaring blaze, the vast royal archives—records that stretched back to the founding of the realm—crumbled to ash. Screams rose and fell, muffled by the wind and smoke, the voices of soldiers, servants, perhaps even nobles, lost to the chaos.

Still, Cade did not move. The city behind him had fallen silent, as though stunned by the violence of its own unmaking. Bethos, the orderly, the ancient, the proud, was unraveling. And above it all, the heavens remained closed, the stars gone as if unwilling to witness the end.

Beside him, Falco's knuckles whitened around the hilt of his sword. "This isn't an accident," he muttered.

Cade nodded, his gaze fixed on the collapsing spire. "No. It feels... orchestrated."

A sudden explosion sent a shockwave through the air, and a section of the palace wall crumbled, sending debris cascading into the courtyard. Screams echoed, a cacophony of panic and despair.

From the chaos emerged General Vladrin, his armor scorched, a gash bleeding across his brow. He barked orders, rallying the guards, his voice a beacon amidst the turmoil.

"Secure the perimeter! No one enters or leaves!"

Cade and Falco descended the wall, weaving through the throng of soldiers and civilians. Smoke choked the air, and the cries of the wounded mingled with the clash of steel and the hiss of flame. They reached Vladrin as he surveyed the devastation, his face grim, his hands clenched at his sides.

"General," Cade began, struggling to catch his breath, "what happened?"

Vladrin turned, his eyes blazing. "The Greens. They've struck at our heart. The Queen is missing—presumed dead."

Falco stepped forward, wiping soot from his face. "Are we certain it was them?"

Vladrin's gaze hardened. "Who else would dare such an act? They've long coveted our downfall."

Cade exchanged a glance with Falco. The Greens were chaotic, yes, but this attack bore the mark of precision, not madness. Something didn't fit. But there was no time for theories—not yet.

In the days that followed, the city grappled with its loss. The Queen's absence left a void, and whispers filled the streets of betrayal, of war, of the end of Bethos. Mourners gathered at the palace gates. Watchtowers burned through the night. The people waited, fearful, for word—for hope.

Then came the storm.

It began as a distant rumble, a low growl that resonated through the cobblestones. The sky darkened, and rain fell in sheets, drenching the city. Rivers overflowed, streets became canals, and the eastern lands were swallowed by floodwaters. Markets closed. Bridges collapsed. And still, the rain fell, as if the heavens themselves grieved for Bethos.

Cade stood at the edge of the deluge, the water lapping at his boots. He watched as homes were carried away, as families clung to rooftops, as the very earth seemed to weep.

Falco approached, his cloak soaked, his expression grim. "This isn't natural."

Cade nodded. "It's as if the land itself is mourning."

They returned to the palace ruins, seeking answers amidst the rubble. In the Queen's private chamber, they found a hidden compartment, revealing a journal bound in crimson leather.

Cade opened it, and the pages were filled with elegant script. He read aloud:

"The tredaphor stirs. I feel its pull, its promise. But at what cost? The dreams grow stronger, the voices louder. They speak of fire and flood, of a kingdom reborn through destruction."

Falco's brow furrowed. "She knew."

Cade closed the journal. "She was preparing for something. Perhaps she tried to stop it—and paid the price."

As the city struggled to recover, General Vladrin seized control, declaring martial law. He rallied the army, preparing for war against the Greens.

But Cade and Falco sensed a deeper threat, one that transcended political rivalries. The tredaphor—a force of prophecy and power—loomed over them, its influence seeping into dreams and reality alike.

They met in secret, joined by Travis and Multir, forming a pact to uncover the truth.

"We must find the source," Cade said. "Before the kingdom tears itself apart."

Falco nodded. "Then we journey east, to the heart of the Greens' territory. To the place where the land speaks."

Roger Batista

And so, under the cover of darkness, they set forth, leaving behind a city in turmoil, chasing whispers and shadows, seeking the light hidden within the storm.

Chapter 5 – Threads of the Old Guard

The candlelight in the stone chamber flickered like a heartbeat, casting shifting shadows along the walls and floor. The room was still, save for the soft rustle of fabric as Travis adjusted his position. He knelt before the old tapestry, its colors muted by age but its texture rich with meaning. His gloved fingers moved slowly, reverently, tracing the intricate woven patterns with care and precision. "It's not just decorative," he muttered, more to himself than to anyone else.

Multir stood nearby, arms crossed, leaning against the cold stone wall. His eyes were narrowed with suspicion or thought—it wasn't clear which. "You've said that four times," he remarked, a hint of impatience in his tone.

"And I'll say it a fifth if I must," Travis replied without looking up. His voice was steady, focused. "Look closer. This pattern here—see how it repeats? But every sixth stitch breaks form. It's deliberate."

He tapped lightly at the deviation, drawing Multir's attention to the subtle inconsistency. There was an underlying structure, a message perhaps, woven into the fabric. The tapestry wasn't simply art—it was information, hidden in plain sight, waiting to be understood by those who knew how to look.

The cloth was massive—nearly ten feet wide—and older than the palace itself. It hung in one of the forgotten halls beneath the old archives, where dust lay thick on the shelves, undisturbed, like the silence of forgotten centuries. The threads depicted a sweeping panorama of the Eight Kingdoms: mountains traced in silver, rivers etched in blue, and cities glinting faintly with worn gold. Yet it was the lower left corner that drew Travis's eye. There, the threads curled into a spiral of crimson, distinct and unlike anything else in the design, breaking the pattern with quiet defiance.

Multir stepped forward and studied the mark. "Could be damage," he said, though his tone lacked confidence.

"No," Travis replied, already reaching into his satchel. He withdrew a weathered parchment and spread it out carefully. "It's code."

The parchment revealed a faded map scrawled with notes in the Bethan cipher—slanted symbols and markings aligned to hidden trails. Along one edge, the same crimson spiral appeared, drawn in careful ink. Travis pointed to it.

"The Old Guard used textile patterns to pass messages—stitching hidden codes into wall hangings, robes, even cloaks. What we're looking at here was no mere ornament. It was a declaration. A manifesto, written not in ink, but in thread."

Multir let out a slow whistle. "Then this wasn't just a rebellion. It was a movement. With its own structure, rites… even belief."

Travis nodded, his expression tightening with understanding. "And if I'm right, this mark—" he tapped the spiral lightly, "—this speaks of the tredaphor."

His voice fell into a hush, the name carrying weight. In the flickering lamplight, the crimson spiral seemed to shift slightly, like it was waiting to be understood.

That night, Falco awoke breathless, his skin clammy with sweat. The dream had returned—clearer now, more vivid.

He stood in a chamber of velvet darkness. Above him, the tapestry loomed, enormous and alive, the threads slithering like serpents of silk. Men bowed before him, their faces obscured. A voice—female, ancient—spoke from nowhere and everywhere.

"They await the threadbreaker. He who is both end and beginning."

Falco reached toward the tapestry. It pulsed, alive, and his fingers brushed a single golden thread. Instantly, the darkness exploded into light.

He gasped awake.

Outside his tent, the wind howled across the eastern plateau. His small band of companions still slept—Cade, Travis, Multir, and the few who now traveled with them, believing in a prophecy that Falco himself still didn't understand.

He pulled on his cloak and stepped into the moonlight, seeking clarity in the cold.

Cade joined him minutes later, drawn by the sound of Falco pacing.

"Another dream?" Cade asked.

Falco nodded, voice hushed. "The same tapestry. But this time… the thread spoke. Or maybe the voice did. I can't tell anymore."

Cade's gaze was distant. "Dreams don't lie. But they don't always tell the truth, either."

"I don't want to be what they say I am," Falco said. "A symbol. A savior. I'm not built for that."

"You don't have to be. Maybe the tredaphor doesn't need someone to lead... just someone to listen."

The next morning, Travis gathered the group inside a ruined watchtower at the edge of Bethan territory. "I've confirmed it," he said, excitement cracking through his calm demeanor. "The tapestry holds a rebel code. And I've translated part of it."

He held up a piece of vellum.

"In the thread is the sword. In the sword is the truth. In truth, the silent flame."

"What does that mean?" asked Multir.

"It's part of the Old Guard's doctrine," Travis explained. "They believed truth wasn't something you found. It was something you forged. And the tredaphor—whatever it is—was the key to forging it."

Falco frowned. "You think the tapestry leads us to it?"

"More than that," said Travis. "I think it does. Or at least, part of it."

Cade stepped forward. "If the tapestry's language is metaphorical, we have to think like them. The 'thread' isn't just a thread. It's lineage. Fate. Choice."

Multir nodded. "And the 'sword' could mean action... or sacrifice."

Falco felt the pressure mounting in his chest. "So then what am I? The threadbreaker? The sword?"

Silence settled, heavy and uncertain.

Travis finally said, "Maybe both. Maybe neither. But they wrote about you."

He handed Falco a torn fragment of cloth retrieved from the tapestry's backside. On it was embroidered a figure cloaked in silver, standing at a crossroads between flame and flood. Beneath it, stitched in the script of the Old Guard, were the words:

"He who walks in a dream shall wake the sleeping blade."

Falco stared at it for a long time. "Then I need to go back."

"To the palace ruins?" asked Cade.

"To the tapestry," Falco said. "It's not done speaking."

They returned under the cover of night, sneaking through crumbled walls and flooded courtyards. The ruins of the palace groaned like a dying beast beneath them, but the tapestry remained untouched, waiting.

Falco stood before it and placed his palm on the spiral once more.

This time, something responded.

The spiral shimmered faintly. A hidden latch released with a soft *click*, and part of the wall behind the tapestry slid aside, revealing a narrow passage.

Travis's eyes lit up. "Of course! A double blind. The code was the key."

They followed the corridor into a stone chamber lit by a skylight of green crystal. At the center stood a pedestal—and atop it, a book bound in scales.

Falco approached slowly, heart pounding. He opened it.

Inside were the writings of the Old Guard. Doctrines. Maps. Visions.

And prophecy.

"The tread shall break, the blade shall rise. Brothers, two shall walk the fire. One shall fall by trust, the other by truth. But neither shall die."

Cade read over his shoulder. "This is about us."

Falco felt the weight of the pages. "But why us? Why now?"

Multir pointed to a final line inked in red:

"When flame falls and flood rises, the blade shall find its bearer—one who dreams not only his fate, but all fates."

Travis looked at Falco, voice cautious. "It's you."

In the weeks that followed, whispers spread.

Others joined them—hunters from the woods, exiles from the Greens, wandering priests who claimed the Queen was not dead, only hidden. They came not for the prophecy, but for Falco. Word had traveled. The tapestry had spoken. A new path was forming, one not of monarchs or generals, but of those who believed in something older, deeper.

Falco began to change. Not in power—but in presence. He moved with greater silence, listened longer before speaking, and when he did speak, others followed.

But in private, he unraveled.

Each night, the dreams grew stronger. Sometimes he was a king. Sometimes a killer. Sometimes both. He began to hear the voice even while awake—a whisper in the wind, a murmur in flame.

Cade found him one night at the edge of the river, eyes glassy.

"You're losing sleep," Cade said.

"I'm losing self," Falco replied. "I don't know where the dream ends anymore."

"You're afraid you're just a puppet."

Falco nodded. "A blade in someone else's hand."

Cade sat beside him. "Then be the hand."

Falco blinked. "What?"

"Be the one who chooses—not the one chosen."

Their camp shifted toward the borderlands, closer to the Greens' territory. The land there was strange—trees that pulsed with sound, stones that hummed at night. People called it the Living Verge.

Here, the tapestry's final message would reveal itself.

One morning, a woman arrived—hooded, limping, with a scar across her cheek. She spoke a name no one had uttered in decades.

"I was Old Guard," she said, "before the fall. I watched the Queen rise. I know what the tapestry hid."

They brought her into the tent, and Falco sat before her.

She placed a single object in his palm: a needle of gold.

"The threadbreaker's weapon," she said. "Not sword or spear. Needle. The tool of weavers. The power to choose which threads to cut, and which to mend."

Falco stared at it, mystified.

"This is the tredaphor?" he asked.

The woman smiled. "The tredaphor is not the weapon. It's the weaving. It is the truth you shape, not the one you inherit."

That night, Falco returned to the tapestry in his dreams.

This time, he held the needle.

And the threads no longer slithered—they waited.

He reached forward, chose one, and snipped.

Instantly, a thousand images bloomed before him— visions of countless possible worlds, each branching from the choices made and the paths taken. In some of these worlds, he ruled with unquestioned authority, a sovereign with the power to shape destiny.

In others, he died before ever reaching the throne, his potential lost to time and chance. There were worlds where Cade stood tall on a fragile throne of glass, his reign teetering on the edge of collapse, and others where Travis wept bitterly over a kingdom swallowed by floodwaters, powerless to save what had once been his. Each vision shimmered with its own reality, vivid and undeniable.

Yet amid the chaos of these diverging fates, there was one world that stood apart—where no single person ruled, but rather a circle of leaders guided by unity and shared purpose. That was the future he chose, the one he began to stitch toward with quiet resolve.

Chapter 6 – The Echo Vale

The road heading north stretched out like a narrow ribbon of gray, winding silently through dense forests that seemed to lean inward, their skeletal branches reaching out like fingers. These gnarled limbs whispered secrets in the cold wind—secrets Cade could feel but not yet understand. Above him, the sky was a heavy, dull canvas painted in shades of ash and slate, as if the heavens themselves were holding their breath, waiting for something uncertain to unfold. The air was thick with a quiet tension, a stillness that pressed against Cade's skin and settled deep in his bones. He rode alone, the solitude as heavy as the weight of his mission pressing relentlessly on his shoulders. Each mile carried him further into the unknown, and though the path was clear, the future remained shrouded in shadow. Cade's thoughts were consumed by the gravity of what lay ahead, the burden of purpose driving him onward.

Ahead lay Echo Vale—an ancient name spoken only in hushed tones and riddled with rumors. It was said to be a place where time folded in on itself, where past and future blurred, and where reality became as fluid as water. The legends said those who entered the Vale could glimpse what was, what is, and what might be. But none who ventured there emerged unchanged.

Cade's heart hammered in his chest as he neared the boundary where the trees thinned and the air thickened with an eerie stillness. A mist clung to the ground, swirling around his horse's hooves like living smoke.

As he dismounted, a strange sensation prickled along his spine—a complex mix of anticipation and dread that he could neither fully explain nor resist. The stories he had heard since childhood whispered warnings of Echo Vale's formidable power: it was a place that tested not just the body, but the very essence of the mind and spirit. Those who entered unprepared often found their certainty stripped away, leaving only doubt and shadow in its place. Yet, despite the fear such tales inspired, Cade could not turn back now. The pull of the Vale was something ancient and unyielding, calling him forward with a voice that echoed deeper than any mere sound.

He took a tentative step forward, his boots sinking slightly into the soft earth. Around him, the mist hung thick and heavy, swirling gently in the cool air like breath from another world. The mist seemed to murmur, its soft whispers curling around him in a language older than the kingdoms themselves—words long forgotten by time, spoken in silence and carried on the wind. The atmosphere was thick with unseen eyes, and the air vibrated faintly with the weight of countless unseen watchers.

Deeper into the Vale, Cade's cautious progress brought him to a small clearing where the mist suddenly parted like a heavy curtain drawn aside by unseen hands. In the center stood a simple stone hut, its surface worn and weathered by countless seasons. Vines draped its steep roof in a tangled embrace, while the walls were etched with strange carvings—eyes wide open, ears sharply attuned, and mouths set as if mid-speech. These ancient symbols spoke of watching, listening, and communicating without words—reminders that this place was alive with meanings beyond the surface.

From within the hut came the unmistakable sound of slow, measured breathing, steady and rhythmic like a pulse. Cade approached with utmost caution, every sense alert. When he reached the door, it creaked open on rusted hinges, revealing the figure of an old woman standing there. Her skin resembled cracked parchment, worn thin by time and hardship, while her eyes were milky white, blind, yet somehow seeming to see everything at once.

"I have awaited you," she said, her voice soft and steady, as delicate as the mist that lingered outside.

"Who are you?" Cade asked, his voice barely above a whisper, caught between curiosity and wariness.

"I am Mirana," she replied. "Once, I served the Queen's grandmother—before the flames, before the flood. I am the keeper of truths hidden beneath silence and shadow."

Cade felt his heart quicken with a mixture of awe and urgency. "I seek knowledge of the tredaphor," he said.

Mirana nodded slowly and motioned for him to enter. Inside, the hut was dimly lit by a single oil lamp that cast flickering shadows on the rough stone walls. Shelves lined the room, cluttered with ancient scrolls, bones, and faded relics whose origins were lost to time.

"The tredaphor," Mirana began, her voice low and reverent, "is far more than a mere symbol. It is a weapon— one forged not from steel or fire, but from silence and trust. It cannot be wielded by those who harbor doubt or fear. Only those who believe in its power, unwaveringly, until the very end, can claim its strength."

Cade listened intently, absorbing every word as if it were a lifeline.

"Tell me what you know," he urged, his voice steady but urgent.

Mirana closed her eyes and began to chant softly in the ancient tongue. The room darkened around him, and Cade felt himself begin to drift—pulled inward and downward—into a vision that promised to reveal what lay beyond mortal understanding.

He was standing in a vast throne room, bathed in cold blue light.

At the center of the grand chamber, Falco sat upon a throne hewn from black stone, its surface cold and unyielding beneath him. His white tunic, once pristine, was now stained deeply with blood, the vivid crimson streaming steadily from a wound along his side. Despite the pain that surely coursed through his body, his face remained eerily calm, almost serene, though noticeably pale—his complexion drained of its usual warmth, as if the life was slowly ebbing from him.

Before Falco knelt Cade himself, his form tense and rigid with the weight of the moment. In his hands, he held a dagger, its sharp blade poised dangerously close to Falco's heart, glinting faintly in the dim light. The tension in the room was palpable; silence had fallen like a heavy curtain, thick and suffocating, broken only by the slow, rhythmic drip of blood as it fell drop by drop onto the cold marble floor below.

Then, cutting through the stillness, a voice echoed in the vastness of the chamber—strange and yet hauntingly familiar at the same time, as if it were both distant and intimately known:

"You will follow the wrong one. And still, you will lead."

Cade's hands began to tremble, a subtle but unmistakable quiver betraying the turmoil within. The vision before him shifted suddenly, as if reality itself wavered. Now, Falco stood alone atop a windswept hill, his silhouette stark against a sky ablaze with burning light, fiery hues painting the horizon in ominous reds and oranges. In contrast, Cade watched from the shadows below, hidden and silent.

A second voice whispered, barely audible yet full of weight and meaning:

"Trust is a blade with two edges."

With a start, Cade awoke, his breath coming fast and shallow. Sweat beaded on his brow, cool and clammy against his skin. Nearby, Mirana's eyes opened slowly, revealing milky orbs that pierced through the darkness like pale lanterns. Her voice, soft yet steady, broke the lingering silence:

"The vision you saw is a warning," she said quietly. "It speaks not only of betrayal but also of a destiny intertwined with forces beyond your understanding. The tredaphor is not merely a weapon of war; it is a test of loyalty and faith."

Cade lowered himself heavily onto a low wooden stool, his mind racing to unravel the meaning behind her words. He felt the weight of uncertainty pressing down on him like a physical burden.

"Does this mean I will betray Falco?" he asked, his voice cracking with fear and doubt.

Mirana's gaze did not waver; it remained calm and unwavering as she replied, "It means you must decide who you trust—not just in others, but also in yourself."

Mirana guided Cade through rituals of silence, meditation, and reflection. She showed him the Vale's hidden mirrors—pools of water, shards of obsidian, and polished metal—through which he glimpsed fragments of possible futures.

One afternoon, as Cade stared into a crystal-clear pool, an image formed: a world torn apart by war, with Falco crowned in blood and Cade cast into exile, his heart shattered.

Tears blurred Cade's vision.

"Can this be changed?" he whispered.

Mirana smiled faintly. "The threads are not fixed. The tredaphor is the weaving of fate itself. You have the power to cut and stitch the fabric of what is to come. But it requires courage to face the darkness within."

Cade nodded slowly, feeling the burden grow heavier yet more urgent.

One evening, as the cold Vale mist curled around the hut like a serpent, Cade found himself speaking to Mirana about his doubts and fears.

"I do not understand why Falco—why *he* must carry this burden. And why am I tied to him so tightly?"

Mirana's voice was gentle. "You and Falco are two threads in the same tapestry. One cannot exist without the other. Your choices, your trust, will shape the outcome of the kingdoms' fate."

"But what if I fail him?" Cade's voice cracked with anguish. "What if I become the dagger instead of the shield?"

Mirana leaned forward, placing a withered hand over his.

"The tredaphor is a weapon of silence. It is trust forged in the absence of words, a bond stronger than any blade. If you wield it with truth, it will protect. But if doubt rules you, it will destroy."

The night before he was to leave Echo Vale, Cade sat alone by the fire, staring into the flames. The vision haunted him still—Falco bleeding, the dagger in his hand.

What did it mean? Was it a future already written or a warning yet to be heeded?

He had come seeking answers and instead found more questions.

Suddenly, a whisper drifted on the wind.

"You will follow the wrong one. And still, you will lead."

Cade shivered, the firelight casting long shadows across his face.

He knew one thing: the path ahead would not be simple. It would demand sacrifices, trust, and the courage to walk into darkness—not alone, but with those bound by fate.

At dawn, Cade left the Vale, the mist swallowing his footsteps.

As he rode south toward the unsettled lands of Bethos, his heart was heavy but resolute.

Falco awaited—his friend, his rival, his mystery.

And the tredaphor—the silent weapon—called them both toward a destiny neither fully understood.

The echoes of the Vale followed Cade like a ghost, whispering truths and lies in equal measure.

He could no longer deny the truth of the vision.

He must choose.

Chapter 7 – Dreams in Third Person

The battlefield was a cacophony of clashing steel and anguished cries. Smoke mingled with the blood-soaked earth, stinging eyes, and choking throats. War drums pounded like thunder across the valley, marking the cadence of death. Amidst the chaos, Falco stood firm, his blade a silver blur, dancing with lethal precision. He fought with the instinct of a wolf and the grace of a king, his every strike felling another of General Vladrin's soldiers.

But the tide of battle was turning. Vladrin's forces pressed hard, a relentless wave of iron and fury. Falco could feel it—the pressure mounting, the line breaking. The air was thick with ash and the coppery scent of blood. He lunged, parried, twisted, and turned—but even he could not be everywhere at once.

Suddenly, a searing pain tore through Falco's side. His breath hitched as a spear pierced through his armor, hot blood flooding his tunic. He staggered, vision spinning. The roar of battle faded into a dull throb. Knees buckling, he collapsed, his blade slipping from his grasp. The world dimmed, sounds distorting into echoes. Darkness enveloped him, soft and consuming.

Silence.

Then, a strange awareness.

Falco opened his eyes—not in the battlefield, but in a dreamlike void. He was weightless, a silent observer, removed from the time before him, unfolding a surreal tapestry woven from memories and mysteries.

He saw Cade—his closest companion, his anchor in the storm—wandering through a vast labyrinth shrouded in mist. The stone walls shifted and stretched, impossibly high and cruelly narrow. Cade's steps were slow and hesitant, his eyes darting left and right. Confusion marked his face. Sorrow clung to his features like dew on dying leaves.

"Falco?" Cade's voice echoed into the void, tinged with desperation. "Where are you?"

Falco tried to speak, to call out, but his lips refused to move. He reached forward, but his hands passed through the scene like smoke. He was there, yet not. Powerless.

The vision changed.

Now, Travis stood in a grand hall, columns rising like sentinels around him. He paced, engaged in an invisible battle of intellect and instinct. His eyes darted, reading signs, anticipating moves, countering traps laid by unseen adversaries. Yet, behind him, a long shadow crept—quiet, deliberate. A threat unnoticed.

Next, Multir appeared, kneeling beside a veiled figure. Tears streamed down the warrior's face—Multir, the unshakable, weeping openly. The identity of the figure was hidden, but Falco could feel the gravity of the moment. Grief and reverence pulsed through the air.

Another shift.

Falco now saw himself, draped in regal garb, seated on a grand throne. Blood seeped from a wound at his side, staining the ornate fabric. Cade knelt before him, a dagger in hand. His eyes brimmed with anguish and conflict.

"Is this my fate?" Falco whispered, the weight of destiny pressing like a stone upon his chest.

The vision splintered.

Falco's eyes fluttered open. The battlefield was gone. In its place—dim candlelight, the faint scent of dried herbs, and linen sheets. The chamber was modest yet safe. Bandages wrapped his midsection tightly, the pain a dull reminder of what had happened.

Beside him, Cade sat, his gaze distant, brow furrowed with thought. At the sound of Falco's stirring, his expression changed—first startled, then awash with relief.

"You're awake," Cade said, leaning forward. "Thank the stars."

Falco's voice was rough, strained. "What happened?"

"You were wounded. Badly. Travis held the flank while Multir dragged you out. We made it to an outpost near the river. You've been unconscious for days."

Falco nodded, trying to sit upright. Cade steadied him.

"I saw things," Falco murmured. "Not dreams. Visions. You… Travis… Multir. And someone else. The Queen, maybe. Hidden. Veiled."

Cade nodded in agreement. "I've seen them too. Visions. They feel more real than anything else. Like they're not dreams at all, but messages."

They fell into silence. Something in Cade's presence brought Falco a strange comfort—like peace and strength.

Days passed.

Falco healed slowly, his strength returning like a tide. But the dreams continued, vivid and haunting.

In one, he and Cade stood atop a windswept cliff, the ocean crashing below. Thunder and storm clouds in the distance. Suddenly, a gale pulled Cade into the abyss. In another, the queen led a solemn procession, her presence commanding the reverence of all who watched. Cade and Falco followed, adorned in their finest regalia- symbols of duty, not just rank. Generals and nobles bowed in gratitude, not to them as men, but to the sacrifices they embodied. These visions stirred something in Falco—a truth buried beneath duty and fear.

He remembered childhood nights spent dreaming- not just of power and glory, but also of something quieter. Peace. The unhurried rhythm of country life, where the weight of duty did not shape him, where he was not a warrior or a symbol, just a boy with open skies above him. Would he ever feel that again?

One evening, as the sun dipped low and painted the sky in hues of molten gold, Falco found Cade in the courtyard, tending a falcon perched on his wrist.

"Cade," Falco said.

Cade turned, his features bathed in the orange glow. "You're up."

"I need to talk."

Cade nodded, gesturing to the stone bench nearby. Falco sat beside him, heart pounding.

"It's about the dreams," Falco began, his voice low. "They've shown me things I've tried to ignore."

Cade looked at him, calm but unreadable. "What kind of things?"

Falco hesitated. "That my path… isn't just about prophecy or power. It's about choices. About who I trust. Who I… need by my side."

Cade's expression eased, a knowing look settling in his gaze. "You already know my answer."

One hand found the other's shoulder- a firm press, unspoken trust sealed the gesture.

That night, the dreams returned.

Falco stood on a battlefield again, but this time, Cade was beside him, blade in hand, eyes bright with courage. Behind them, the forces of Bethos rallied—not for a crown, but for a cause. For unity. But something strange happened. Cade raised his hand, and peace and strength washed over the group.

A final vision: the veiled queen unveiled, her face familiar. A reflection of Falco's own fears—an embodiment of fate itself. She was walking with Cade. She looked at Falco, smiled, then vanished like mist.

Falco awoke with a calm heart.

Whatever lay ahead—prophecies, betrayals, battles—whatever lay ahead, he would meet it alongside Cade. Not as a lone figure bound to legend, but as a man guided by another's keen sight-one who saw beyond mere fate.

The line between dream and waking blurred. But one truth remained crystal clear: their bond was unbreakable, destined to shape the future of Bethos.

And perhaps, the fate of the world itself.

Chapter 8 – The Day of Brothers True

The morning sun barely pierced the storm-stained skies above Bethos. Smoke still rose from scattered outposts, and the rivers ran thicker than they should. Men with swords wandered the halls of once-sacred temples, and the bells of the old monastery had long since ceased to toll. Something unnatural had sunk into the bones of the kingdom— something that made even the birds quiet and the wind uncertain.

In the ruined chapel of Varnell, Cade stood alone.

The stained-glass windows above him—once radiant depictions of Adriun's blessing—were blackened from the palace fire. The pews were ash, and yet, in the quiet, Cade felt watched. Not by ghosts, nor gods, but by choice itself. It pressed against his back like an invisible tide, urging him toward the gathering storm.

"It will be today," a voice said softly behind him.

Falco stepped into the ruin, one hand still bandaged from a wound barely healed. He carried no sword—only a carved branch from the whispering trees of Delren Woods, polished into the shape of a staff.

Cade turned. "You walk like it's your last day."

Falco gave a broken smile. "And you speak like you've already seen it."

A silence passed between them. Not cold, not bitter, but full of the things they could not say.

Cade had not told Falco everything—not the full vision from Echo Vale, not the dagger he saw in his own hand, not the pain that flared in his chest whenever Falco spoke too gently. There was something ancient stirring between them, like a tether neither could cut, even if they wished it.

"I dreamt again last night," Cade confessed, eyes flickering to the shattered altar. "But it wasn't my dream. It was... someone else's."

Falco nodded. "I've had them too. Dreams in voices I don't recognize. Sometimes, I think they're yours."

The two stood in the chapel for a long time, surrounded by echoing fragments of a kingdom no longer whole.

Outside, the banners of General Vladrin's army began to line the horizon. They came in ranks of black and red, the iron fists of men who had forgotten the old oaths. Vladrin's proclamation had already reached every town in the realm:

"Bethos must not fall to shadows. I alone have the will to lead. I claim the throne in the Queen's absence—for peace, for strength, for the good of all."

But his peace was soaked in blood.

Cade and Falco mounted horses bred for endurance, not speed, and rode with Travis and Multir to the war table beneath the ancient Elm of Virelle. The trunk had stood for three hundred years; its roots were said to twist through forgotten tombs beneath the earth. There, captains from the outer provinces had begun to gather. Some were loyal to the Queen's vanished name. Others followed Falco, believing the prophecy.

"You'll need to address them," Travis murmured. "They're divided. Even now."

Falco stepped forward. Dust clung to his boots, and his cloak was threadbare from travel.

"I don't ask for crowns," he said, loud enough for all to hear. "Nor do I ask you to follow me blindly, but I believe this land is not yet lost. I believe we are more than pawns in Vladrin's war."

An old knight from the southern coast spat on the ground. "Fine words, but who speaks for the Queen?"

"I do," said a new voice.

Every head turned. The figure who stepped from the shadows wore traveler's garb, dirt-streaked and nondescript. As she approached the table, a hush spread like wildfire.

It was the Queen.

Or rather, it had been.

Her hair, once adorned with gold and silver thread, was tied back simply. Her skin bore lines from the sun and wind. Yet her eyes—those eyes—held the weight of the realm.

"I have walked among you. I have listened, and learned. The court was poisoned. I left to see what remained outside its walls. Now I return not to rule, but to guide."

She looked to Cade and Falco.

"These two were chosen—not by prophecy, but by who they choose to become."

Whispers filled the gathering.

Cade's breath caught. The vision. The dagger. The kneeling. Was this it?

But the Queen was not done.

"I give no orders today," she said. "Only a truth. The Tredaphor is real—but it is not a weapon of steel or fire. It is trust. A choice. A belief carried beyond reason."

Multir stepped beside her, eyes wide with awe. "The Tredaphor… is a person?"

"No," the Queen answered softly. "It is what binds the right ones, even when they are wrong."

With that, she stepped back.

As the sun dipped behind thunderclouds, the battle began.

Vladrin's army struck from the east, flames curling at the edges of the forest as his war engineers set the dry bramble alight. Screams tore through the mist. Falco fought not with rage, but with clarity. Each motion was deliberate, almost graceful, as if he moved in time with something invisible.

Cade found himself drawn to the center of the field. Arrows hailed overhead. Travis barked commands through a broken horn. Multir fought beside the Queen herself, defending her as she refused to retreat.

Then Cade saw him—Vladrin.

Clad in a breastplate of crimson-black, eyes burning with conviction, he carved through loyalists like a man possessed. Although it wasn't until he struck down a messenger boy that Cade felt it—the moment snapped.

He ran.

Falco was already moving toward Vladrin, but something wasn't right. Cade could feel it in his chest—as if time itself had slowed.

The battlefield blurred. Sounds twisted.

Cade saw the image again: Falco on the throne. Blood dripping from his side. Cade on his knees, a dagger in his hand. But this time, something changed.

He wasn't holding the blade to strike.

He was handing it over.

"Take it," Cade said, breathless, as he reached Falco amidst the chaos.

Vladrin raised his sword.

Falco caught the dagger from Cade's outstretched hand.

In one motion—without fury, without glory—he plunged it into Vladrin's side.

The general staggered, disbelieving. "You... no... You're just boys…"

"Then you should've feared us more," Falco whispered.

The battle ended not in triumph, but in silence.

Men stopped fighting. The Queen emerged, her cloak soaked from rain and blood, and walked across the battlefield like a mother searching for her sons.

When she reached Cade and Falco, she knelt with them, touching each of their foreheads.

"It is done," she said.

But was it?

That night, fires burned high across Bethos—not of war, but of memory. The dead were honored. The wounded tended.

In the quiet moments that followed, Cade stood beneath the Elm of Virelle again, staring into a pool of water that had collected at the base of its roots.

His reflection shimmered. Falco stood behind him.

"I thought I was supposed to lead," Cade said softly.

"You did," Falco replied.

"I thought I was supposed to kill you."

Falco chuckled faintly. "So did I. Maybe we both were wrong."

A pause.

Then Cade turned. "In all those dreams, all those visions... I never saw the part where you looked at me like that."

Falco's gaze was unreadable. "Like what?"

"Like you already knew what I would do."

Falco stepped closer.

"I've always known. You are who you are," he said. Falco's smile turned wide. "The best of us. The best of Bethos. Ask the queen."

Cade shook his head as if to say no as a smile cracked his face. Cade, suddenly, punched Falco on the shoulder. Falco winced, not so much from the pain, but from the shock. He laughed as he grabbed his shoulder.

"Now that's new!" said Falco in a surprised tone. Their laughs faded into the forest echoes.

In the soft mist beneath the ancient tree, no one spoke for a long time.

Only the wind replied, whispering a riddle neither of them yet understood.

Far away, in a forgotten glen, an old tapestry shivered on its frame. The threads pulsed—just once—with a heartbeat, neither of them heard.

But the Tredaphor was listening.

Chapter 9 – The Mirror of Destiny

Morning came with an uncanny stillness, the kind that settles not in celebration but in the echo of something broken. The fall of Vladrin had sent tremors through the land, and now the air itself seemed hesitant to move. It was not the hush of triumph, but a brittle quiet, fragile as glass, as if the very soul of Bethos paused to listen for what might come next. People rose early, not out of routine but compulsion, drawn by an invisible tension that threaded itself through the streets and alleyways.

In Fenwall's marketplace, the usual clamour of barter and trade was absent. Instead, a different kind of gathering formed—silent, attentive, and pulsing with anticipation. The townsfolk, young and old, converged not for spices or cloth, but for confirmation of a whisper that had taken root in the night: that someone had come.

Among the crowd, a cloaked woman moved—not remarkable in appearance, but radiant in the serenity she carried. Her presence seemed to calm the air around her. With quiet dignity, she placed hands on shoulders, offered soft-spoken answers, and listened more than she spoke.

Then, just as quietly as she came, she slipped away—swallowed again by the crowd, leaving awe in her wake.

Until Falco and Cade found her.

They caught sight of her near the central well—linen shawl over her braid, dust on her boots, laughter in her eyes. Falco's breath stuttered. Cade's heart pounded an echo of resonance he couldn't name.

"Your Grace?" he whispered, incredulously.

She smiled, fingertips brushing Cade's arm as he reached to steady her. "Did you truly not recognize me?"

Falco's cloak whipped in the breeze. "We heard you were... gone." His voice faltered on the word.

She laughed softly. "I was avoiding the throne. Watching. Learning. Seeing how the people lived, suffered, hoped."

Travis and Multir pushed through the crowd to their side. "You've been living here?" Travis demanded, equally amazed and relieved.

"In silence," the Queen replied. "Until the time was right."

Later, in the courtyard, where benches were arranged in a wide circle, and the air was perfumed with the slow-burning smoke of sacred herbs rising from ceremonial fires, the Queen sat quietly between Falco and Cade. The smoke drifted around them in soft coils, sanctifying the gathering space as if to cleanse the old and bless what was beginning. Around them, the newly formed council—composed of merchants who had once feared taxation, scholars who had preserved truth in secret, farmers whose fields had survived the war, and soldiers who had laid down arms—waited in silence, their eyes fixed on the Queen, uncertain of what the future might hold.

Falco, who had spent most of the day silent and braced against the stone wall for strength, finally found his footing. His voice, steady and resolute, cut through the hush. "Your Majesty," he said, turning toward her, "the kingdom looks to you now. Will you rule?"

The Queen looked out at the circle and slowly shook her head, her expression serene but unyielding. "I will not rule—not as before," she said. "The throne belongs to no one person. It was never meant to contain a people's hope or carry the burden of every dream. We have seen the cost when power is centralized. We must not forget."

A ripple of murmurs stirred among the council members, some nodding, others exchanging glances. Cade leaned forward, his brows furrowed in thought. "So the council holds power?" he asked. "The Tredaphor... it becomes a symbol of unity, not dominion. We reject inheritance, so others may choose freely?"

The Queen's eyes shone with quiet conviction. "Exactly," she replied. "The real hero isn't the one who takes power—but the one who refuses it, so others may rise."

That afternoon, outside the gates, a grand ceremony unfolded. People stood in silence as Queen Mirelin approached a broken statue of Vladrin—his armor dented, his face carved with arrogance. She placed a hand on the stone man's shoulder, whispered a blessing, then turned and faced the crowd.

"Let his downfall remind us: no man is above the will of the people." Her voice, calm yet resonant, carried farther than any trumpet's flourish.

Behind the statue, Cade and Falco knelt side by side. Falco's hand rested on Cade's shoulder.

"For unity," Cade said, raising his hand. Falco mirrored him. "For trust."

Together, the gesture ignited the crowd—cheers rose, songs began, and little children danced around them.

Inside the old palace, newly repurposed as the Council Chamber, the Queen presided over the first meeting. The long hall bore banners of all eight kingdoms—symbols of reclaimed harmony. Pillars glowed with firelight and hope.

Falco leaned close to Cade. "Remember what Mirana said? The Tredaphor can't be claimed."

Cade nodded. "And yet here we are—guardians of something forged in silence."

Travis tapped pensively on parchment. "We need laws, systems. But we also need reminders of why they exist. Story. Heart."

Multir, seated opposite, added thoughtfully, "Remembrance. Grace. Empathy."

The Queen motioned forward. "The first task: appoint ambassadors to rebuild relations with the Greens," she said. "But each ambassador must right a wrong done in their name. Each must carry a symbol of trust."

Cade caught the Queen's eye. Beneath the crust of rebuilding lay soft soil—ready for seeds.

That night, Cade and the Queen walked the castle terraces, their breaths misting in the cool air.

"You have altered everything," Cade said softly.

The Queen nodded, her gaze steady. "We have altered it. Together."

Moonlight spilled across their path. Cade closed his eyes. "I believed destiny required sacrifice. I feared I would lose everything."

The Queen's expression softened. "You preserved what was essential."

They stood in silence, a fragile miracle of shared breath.

"Whatever comes next," Cade said, "I simply wish to remain here."

The Queen smiled, quiet as dawn. "As do I."

Falco approached, his presence a comforting familiarity. "The night is growing colder. Shall we return inside?"

Cade and the Queen exchanged a brief, understanding glance before following Falco back into the warmth of the castle.

Days passed, and the council's work took root. Trade routes re-opened. Grain and supplies moved south. The Greens responded—tentative at first, then with cautious warmth. Envoys came bearing gifts: woven silk, carved wood, and living seeds.

From across the kingdom, small rebellions found peace. Soldiers laid armor aside. Ploughmen hoed fields. Teachers returned to classrooms.

Amid it all, the Queen often sat quietly, observing. Falco and Cade stood beside her by the palace windows, watching life rekindle.

"You two are the living tredaphor," the Queen said one afternoon, placing warm hands on their shoulders. "You're proof that unity lives in sacrifice, not conquest."

Cade shifted. "We were just doing what was right."

She smiled, blessing those words. "Then trust in that. It's the most powerful thing you know."

In quiet moments, though, both men recalled darker truths.

Falco: the blade he almost claimed in his dream. Cade: the dagger he held, the choice he almost made. The memory hovered like a shadow over their shared nights.

In those moments, they feared the wound they'd seen might still surface—even as hope warmed the world.

One dawn, in the flooded eastern fields, a messenger arrived. He wore Council colors and carried a sealed letter.

Falco opened it.

It read: "A threat gathers in the Greens. The land itself calls for warriors. Will you stand with us?"

Cade read over his shoulder. "The land calls."

Falco folded the letter. "Then we go."

That afternoon, the council reconvened. The Queen rose, placing a hand on their joined shoulders before speaking.

"No one is Lord of Bethos," she said. "But as guardians of this age, you both hold our future in your hearts."

Then she set the question before them: "Will you answer the Vale's call—to stand with the Greens in unity, not war?"

Falco swallowed. Cade gave him a reassuring nod.

"We will," Cade said.

Falco nodded in agreement.

The Queen looked to the assembled council. "Then it is decided. The next chapter begins—not with swords, but with trust."

The council members began discussing strategies to ensure the success of their mission. The Queen moved around the table, her gaze occasionally lingering on Cade.

As she passed by him, she softly touched his hand, a gesture unnoticed by the others but felt by Cade.

Falco turned to Cade. "Our priority should be securing the northern borders."

Cade nodded. "Agreed. We must also maintain open supply lines."

The Queen glanced at Cade again, her eyes conveying a silent message. As the meeting concluded, she approached Cade, and as they left the chamber, she stole a surprised kiss from him behind a curtain, a fleeting moment of connection.

That night, Falco and Cade stood by the same well in Fenwall. The moon was full, reflecting in its depths.

Falco turned to Cade. "We need to finalize our plans for the northern borders."

Cade nodded. "Yes, and ensure our supply lines remain secure."

They blessed themselves with the water, the coolness, a reminder of the tasks ahead.

And somewhere beneath the surface, the Tredaphor shimmered like a pulse.

Chapter 10 – Salvation or Weapon

The smell of damp earth and fresh hope drifted across the courtyard as the new Council of Bethos gathered beneath a sky the color of pale flax. Gone were royal banners, replaced by woven tapestries representing each of the eight kingdoms—symbols of unity born from chaos. The war's embers had cooled, but the story of what came after was just beginning.

At the center of the circle sat Queen Mirelin—no longer crowned, but still carrying presence. Beside her stood Falco and Cade, their expressions belied by the weight of what had come before. Falco's once-bright armor had been replaced by plain traveling garb; Cade wore the simple sash of a council envoy. Across the circle, voices stirred with expectation.

Mirelin rose. She let her gaze land first on Falco, then Cade, her shoulders stiff with purpose.

"Today, we choose not a ruler," she began, voice steady, "but a purpose. Our kingdom will have no monarch, no throne, and no claimant of power. We stand together—through council, through consensus, through trust."

A murmur rippled through the assembly: craftsmen, scholars, village elders, former soldiers. A council composed not of nobility, but of those who had weathered the fire and flood. All eyes rested on Falco.

Falco stepped forward, chest tight but resolve clear. He raised his voice so every ear could hear.

"When we fought, I believed the sword could free us. But the greatest victories lay in your hands—in your hearts. I refuse the throne because I refuse to be separated from you. I believe in your will, your wisdom." He looked around. "If you trust me, trust that I will stand with you—but not above you."

Silence. And then a single clap—slow, deliberate—from Cade. Others followed. Encouraged, Falco nodded his thanks.

"You saved them," Cade said aloud, his tone quiet but firm. "Not by the blade, but by faith."

Falco turned to Cade: "Your faith steadied me."

Mirelin raised her hand. "Hear these words: Let no man bear authority alone. Let no weapon define our future. Let trust, not tyranny, shape Bethos."

From the back, an elderly farmer spoke: "So no one rules? How do we defend ourselves?"

Multir answered: "The Council stands as defense— diverse voices, tempered by experience. We stand guard over our people together."

Cade added: "We'll maintain a guard—by volunteers. A promise, not a command."

Mirelin gathered her resolve. "We seal this day not with swords or crowns, but with symbol." She stepped forward and placed a battered piece of the Tredaphor casing on the central stone altar. It had burned at the end of the war; scarce and cracked now, but still there.

"This," she said softly, "reminds us of what we once feared—and of what we chose not to become."

Travis, standing beside her, held a handful of wildflower seeds. He released them, letting them fall onto the cracked stone and the casing alike. The flowers would grow—quiet, living symbols of hope.

A hush fell over the council—awed and solemn. When voices resumed, they spoke not as nobles or soldiers, but as citizens united.

In the days that followed, Falco and Cade kept their promise. They roamed the streets of reclaimed towns—talking, listening, planting seeds both literal and metaphorical. They surveyed the rebuilding of roads, reopened schools, and gifted seeds to farmers who had lost everything. They traveled across former battlefields, now dotted with crosses and quiet offerings.

On a sunny morning in the Greenlands, a small girl tugged on Falco's tunic.

"Are you a hero?" she asked, solemn as a priestess.

Falco knelt. "A hero? No. But I woke up one day and found that people needed something bigger than me." He handed her a stick, carved by woodworkers as a gift. "This—this reminds me of their strength." She smiled, eyes bright as dawn.

Cade watched from a distance, heart warm.

Later, at a riverside town, Cade stood among villagers rebuilding a broken dam. A weary mother approached him, clutching her children.

"Your efforts feed us," she said. "But what if stones fail again?"

Cade knelt, too. "Then we rebuild together. With your ideas, your sweat, your voices. We're in this together."

She nodded, comforted.

From the windows of the travelers' lodgings, the queen watched from afar—her people were no longer subjects, but fellow witnesses to a fragile rebirth.

But peace bore its own perils. Tensions smoldered in some corners—small enclaves where warfare had been worshiped. General Vladrin's remnants lingered there, murmuring of lost honor. Traders were ambushed; herders complained of rustled flocks. Falco and Cade investigated quietly—eschewing force.

They found a band of former legionnaires holed in the foothills. Falco walked straight in, unaccompanied. The men drew blades; Falco disarmed them with soft words.

"Is your honor so fragile it breeds violence? Or can you lay down your arms and stand as your own salvation?"

They lowered swords. Cade followed in with food and blankets. In the council's name, they offered land, reparations, and futures outside their past. The men accepted. They joined volunteer guards, working roads—shifting from casualties of war to pillars of peace.

By midsummer, fields were green, rivers clean, and the chatter across taverns spoke of councils, not crowns. Songs replaced marching music. Lilies bloomed where orange fire once flickered. Bethos, battered, was healing.

One evening, under an olive sky, Falco and Cade walked into the Queen's temporary chamber, finding her bent over plans.

"You two look like proud fathers," Mirelin teased, eyes soft.

Falco shook his head. "More like witnesses."

Cade smiled. "I brought you something."

He reached into his satchel and pulled out the fragment of Tredaphor stone—small, gray, but still pulsing if you held it close.

"It's been in council meetings," Cade explained. "But I thought the Council could choose better."

Mirelin regarded it. "We've learned from it. We've lived past it."

Falco took the fragment. It was inert—but warm in his palm.

"Let it remind us," he said, "that power is not what we do with it—but what we refuse to do with it."

The Queen nodded. "May we never forget this lesson."

They passed the stone between them—no throne, no title, just shared conviction.

In the west, a traveler in a hooded cloak arrived in Fenwall's market square. He spoke to the crowd: "They said the Tredaphor was a weapon. But it became a promise. They said the sword would rule. But instead, they offered their hands."

The villagers listened, drawn by his words. A child asked: "Who was the hero?"

The cloaked man gestured at Falco and Cade, who'd come to watch from the edge of the crowd. "Heroes? Perhaps. But the real hero is harder to name."

He lifted his hood, revealing an ordinary face—an envoy from one of the eight kingdoms.

He looked at the crowd.

"Tell me, who did you think the hero was?"

A farmer answered: "The Queen! She refused the throne."

Another: "Falco—he laid down the sword."

A third: "Cade—he built bridges, not walls."

The envoy smiled. "All true. But the hero isn't just one of them—it's the people who stood, chose, and built anew."

That night, around communal fires, the Council drafted laws of fairness, representation, and mutual respect. They spoke most of unity, consultation, and accountability. The Tredaphor's fragment lay at the center—stone of memory, not weapon of might.

Falco and Cade sat side by side, watching embers dance.

"Do you ever wonder," Cade said softly, "If we'll slip back?"

Falco didn't answer at first. Then, placing a hand on Cade's shoulder, he said: "Not if we keep trusting. Not if we never forget what we chose."

Cade raised his hand and gestured to himself and Falco. "Then we're not rulers. We're reminders."

Falco smiled at their reflection in the Council's tablet.

A month later, the envoy convened gatherings across the eastern border—Greens and Bethans listening side by side. The envoy began again: "The hero was not one man, but many."

He held up the stone fragment. "This saved them not by the sword, but by faith."

The people cheered, eyes bright. A banner proclaimed: *Faith Above Force*.

Falco stood beside Cade and Mirelin, tears glistening—not tears of grief, but of gratitude.

At the day's end, they returned to the emptied castle terrace. Moonlight draped across broken ruins—no thrones, no regalia, only open stone. They walked in silence.

Falco looked at Cade. "Thank you, brother—for trusting me when I doubted."

Cade stepped forward and grabbed his shoulders. "You became the hero, not because you held a sword, but because you held faith."

Falco smiled. "And thank you—for holding to the Council when I was tempted to abandon it."

They stood there, the air warm with silence.

Mirelin joined them. She placed her arms around both.

"You two embody the Tredaphor now," she said, voice proud. "Not what it could destroy—but what it could redeem."

Falco raised the fragment. "To unity."

Cade nodded. "To trust."

Mirelin added: "To Bethos."

They stood together, the three of them—no crowns, no throne, only conviction.

The following morning, the Council met again. Business to tend—recovery, peacemaking, laws.

Falco and Cade stayed behind, stepping into the quiet courtyard.

Falco bent to touch a tulip planted by children near the old well. "I think I finally understand."

Cade watched him. "Tell me."

"That the greatest weapon is what we refuse to use."

Cade smiled, warm and certain.

Falco looked ahead. "Thanks to you, the others and the queen. I mean Mirelin. If I must be called a hero—or leader—know I earned it because all of you never let me be alone."

In silence came the acknowledgment.

Later that evening, Falco walked to the farthest battlements. He looked out over fields and towns now lit by lanterns—not alarms. He placed the Tredaphor fragment in his palm, and felt its weight.

"No sword needed," he whispered. "Only faith."

He tucked it into his pouch.

As the gates of the city creaked open, the two old friends stood side by side, cloaks dusted from the long road, eyes scanning the skyline once dominated by the royal spires. Where once flew the monarch's banner, now hung the crest of the Council—equal parts in its familiarity.

Falco let out a low whistle. "Hard to believe, isn't it? We left boys in the service of the Queen. Now we return to a realm ruled by quorum."

Cade gave a quiet nod, the corner of his mouth lifting. "Still feels like home though. Or maybe it's just because you're still here, dragging your boots like a lost hound."

A laugh broke between them, easy as it had always been.

They passed through the square, once a place for royal edicts, now filled with bustling townsfolk debating policy, news, and the rhythm of a people shaping their own fate.

"We have seen the kingdom's transition," Falco murmured.

Cade shrugged. "And arrived just in time for something better to begin."

And together, they walked on—not as soldiers of a crown, but as brothers in a new age.

At dawn, Falco and Cade arrived at the doorstep of the Olive Vale—their childhood home. Its door creaked on mossy hinges; vines curled around walls.

They stood. Watching. Remembering.

Falco said, voice echoing in the stillness: "Home— never left."

Cade smiled. "Always here."

They slept like stones.

When they emerged, eyes half-closed in the rising sun, they shared a soft laugh.

Falco drew in a deep breath. "No throne. No crown."

Cade nodded. "No sword."

They walked inside, ready to live not as rulers, but as two men bound by trust—the living testament to a heroism they never claimed.

But for Cade, there remained a question he could not answer…. "What about Mirelin? Did her kiss mean more than it should?"